The Goose that Laid the Golden Eggs

and other Aesop's Fables

Compiled by Vic Parker

Miles Kelly

First published in 2013 by Miles Kelly Publishing Ltd
Harding's Barn, Bardfield End Green, Thaxted, Essex, CM6 3PX, UK

2 4 6 8 10 9 7 5 3 1

Publishing Director Belinda Gallagher
Creative Director Jo Cowan
Editorial Director Rosie McGuire
Designer Joe Jones
Production Manager Elizabeth Collins
Reprographics Stephan Davis, Jennifer Hunt, Thom Allaway

ISBN 978-1-84810-938-4

Printed in China

British Library Cataloguing-in-Publication Data
A catalogue record for this book is available from the British Library

ACKNOWLEDGMENTS
The publishers would like to thank the following artists who have contributed to this book:
Cover: Frank Endersby
Advocate Art: Natalie Hinrichsen, Tamsin Hinrichsen
The Bright Agency: Marcin Piwowarski
Frank Endersby
Marco Furlotti
Jan Lewis (decorative frames)

Made with paper from a sustainable forest

www.mileskelly.net   info@mileskelly.net

www.factsforprojects.com

Contents

The Deer and the Vine

A deer was once running for his life from some huntsmen. He plunged into a field and, feeling his limbs growing tired, looked desperately for somewhere to hide. He saw a thick vine growing nearby and raced behind it to take cover. Trying to calm his labored breathing, he stood stone-still

as the huntsmen raced past his hiding place – with no idea that the deer was there.

The deer waited for a while, then supposing all danger to be over, he began to munch on the leaves of the vine for refreshment. Little did he know that the huntsmen were not as far away as he thought. One keen-eyed hunter noticed the leaves of the vine moving, although there was no wind. He realized that an animal was hidden there and shot an arrow into the foliage.

The deer was pierced in the heart, and, as he died, he said, "I deserve my fate for feeding upon the leaves of my protector."

Ungratefulness sometimes brings its own punishment.

The Two Neighbors

Long, long ago, in the early days of the world, two neighbors prayed to the great god Zeus, who ruled over the Earth. The neighbors presented gifts and bowed low to the ground. Then they begged Zeus, who was all-knowing and all-powerful, to grant them their hearts' desires.

Zeus looked deep inside them and saw that one of the neighbors burned with a terrible greed, which could never be fulfilled. And Zeus saw that the heart of the other neighbor was on

fire with envy. So to teach them both a lesson, the wise god decided that he would grant each man whatever he wished for himself, but on one condition – the other neighbor would get twice as much.

After the two neighbors had prayed, they began to wish for their hearts' desires, to see if Zeus had heard and answered them.

The first neighbor shut himself inside his house and wished for a room filled with gold. Imagine his astonishment when it appeared before him! But his delight was short-lived, for a few minutes later his neighbor came running to his door to tell him that two rooms of gold had appeared in his house.

7

Of course, this man quickly became unhappy too. Instead of being pleased that he had double the treasure, he was envious that his neighbor had been answered by Zeus and had any treasure at all. He instantly found himself wishing that his greedy neighbor might lose one of his eyes. Of course, it was no sooner said than done – but he himself lost both, and became totally blind.

Vices are their own punishment.

The Hare and the Tortoise

A hare was once boasting to the other animals about how speedy he was.

"No one is faster than me," he said with a smirk. "I challenge anyone to prove me wrong – who is bold enough to race with me?"

Of course, no one dared put themselves forward, until a tortoise slowly lifted his head and spoke. "I accept your challenge," the old, wrinkled one announced softly.

The hare burst out laughing. "Oh, that is funny, please tell me you are joking."

But the tortoise was deadly serious. "Save your boasting until you've beaten me," he said.

The other animals, astonished, rushed to set a course. It took the tortoise several minutes to amble to the start line. Some of the animals muttered to each other and shook their heads.

"Ready, set, go!" bellowed the ox – and finally the race began.

The hare darted out of sight. But as soon as he had rounded the bend, he thought he'd have a laugh at the tortoise's expense. He lay down under a tree and pretended to nap – just to show that he

could even stop to sleep and still beat the tortoise. But in the peaceful coolness, the hare really did fall fast asleep!

Slowly, slowly, the tortoise plodded on – past the sleeping hare – until the finish line was in sight. All at once the hare woke with a start, horrified. He bounded away, but the tortoise passed the finish line before he could catch up.

Slow and steady wins the race.

The Serpent and the File

One hot day, a snake was slithering along, going nowhere in particular, when it glided into the workshop of a craftsman who made armor. The workshop was cool and shady and the snake slid further in, looking for a safe corner in which to curl up and rest.

As it slithered over the floor, it suddenly felt its skin scratched by a rough tool called a file, which the

workman had left lying on the ground. In a rage, the snake turned on it and tried to pierce the iron file with its fangs – but all it succeeded in doing was hurting its mouth.

It is a waste of time to get angry about unfeeling things.

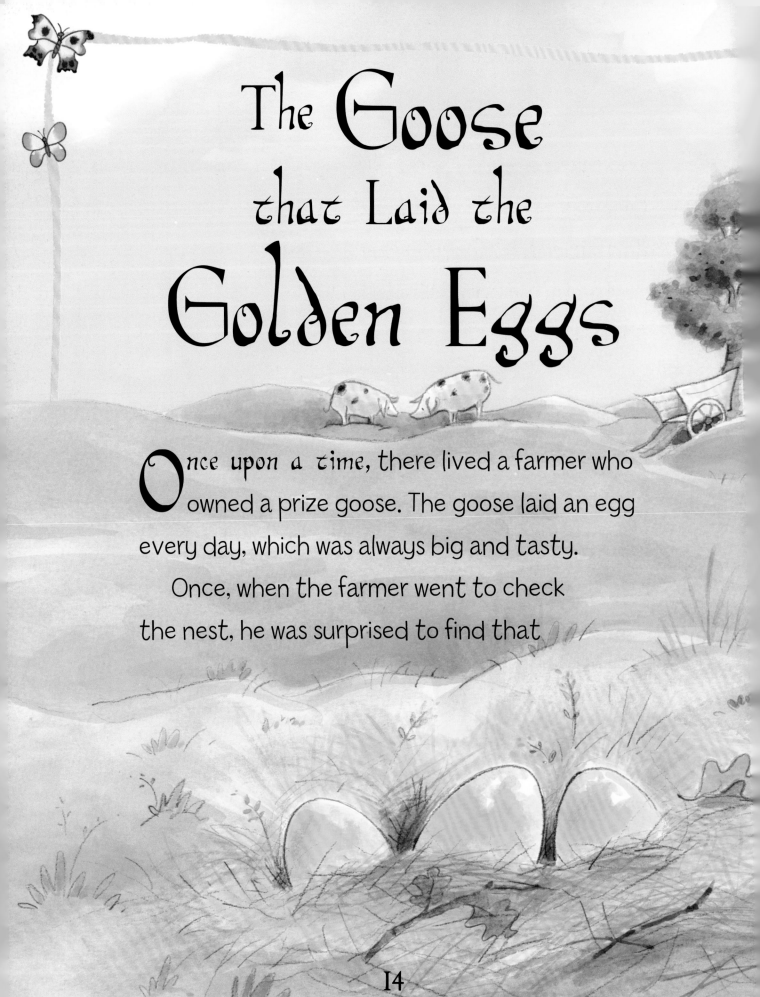

The Goose that Laid the Golden Eggs

Once upon a time, there lived a farmer who owned a prize goose. The goose laid an egg every day, which was always big and tasty. Once, when the farmer went to check the nest, he was surprised to find that

14

the egg looked strange — it was yellow and shiny. When he picked it up, it was as heavy as lead.

The farmer's first thought was that an envious neighbor must have played a trick on him. But just before he threw the egg away, he thought better of it, and took it home instead. There, he examined it closely, and to his surprise he found that the egg was made of pure gold.

To the farmer's amazement, the next day the goose laid another golden egg... and the next day... and the next... He soon became wealthy from selling them. However, as he grew richer, he became greedier. One day he decided he had to have all the gold the goose must have inside her – so he killed her and opened her up, only to find nothing.

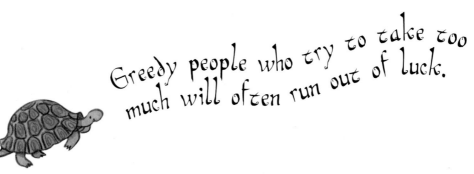

Greedy people who try to take too much will often run out of luck.

The Mischievous Dog

A man once had a dog that was a faithful, loyal companion to him. However, whenever visitors came to the man's house, the dog would bark and snap at them for no reason. The man of course found this a great nuisance — not to mention a danger — so he fastened a bell around the dog's neck. This way, as people approached his house, they would hear the dog

coming and be warned to stay back.

The dog was very proud of the bell. He strutted about tinkling it with great satisfaction, showing it off as if it were a medal.

One day an old dog came up to him and said, "The fewer airs you give yourself the better, my friend. You don't think, do you, that your bell was given as a reward of merit? On the contrary, it is a badge of disgrace."

Notoriety is often mistaken for fame.

The Miser and his Gold

Once upon a time there lived a miserly man, whose greatest pleasure in life was to save his money and count it. Each day, he would lock the door to his house, draw the blinds, and fetch the chest of gold coins from under his bed. His eyes would glint and gleam as he placed the money into piles and counted up the total.

One day, as the man was counting the coins, an awful thought took hold of him. What if someone broke into his house one day while he was at market? They would surely look under the bed and find his treasure. But the old miser could not think of a better hiding place.

Then an idea came to him. "I know," he said to himself, "if there is not a better hiding place inside the house, perhaps outside the house would be safer."

That night, under cover of darkness, the man crept into his garden with a big spade. At the foot of the biggest tree he dug a deep hole, in which he placed his chest of gold. He covered the chest over with earth, then he crept back inside, rubbing his hands with glee.

From then on, every night, the man would steal into his garden and dig up the chest.

He would delight in counting the coins, then bury his treasure in the hole once more. The man thought he had been so clever — no one would come across it there.

However, little did the man know that on one particular night, a robber was hiding in the tree. He saw everything, and of course, as soon as the miser had returned inside his house, the robber came down from the tree, dug up the treasure and ran off with it.

The next night, when the man came outside to gloat over his treasure, he was horrified to find nothing but the empty hole. He wailed and wept and tore at his hair, and raised such an outcry that all his neighbors came running to see what had happened. Then the man owned up and told them about how he used to come and check on his gold.

"Did you ever spend any of it?" asked one neighbor.

"No," said the man, "I only counted it."

"Then come again and look at the hole," said a neighbor, "it will do you just as much good."

 If you don't use wealth and treasures, they may as well not exist.

The Olive Tree
and the
Fig Tree

High on a hillside in a sunny country, an olive tree lived next to a fig tree. They had been neighbors for a long time, putting forth harvest after harvest of fruit. As the two stood surveying the landscape before them, they would chat. From time to time they would tease each other.

One day, the olive tree taunted the fig tree about how she lost her leaves every autumn.

"You lose your leaves each year when the weather turns colder, and you stay bare until

the spring. Whereas I, as you see, stay green all year round." For of course, olive trees are evergreen.

It wasn't long after that the frosts of winter came. The weather was harsh and there was a heavy fall of snow. The snow settled on the tiny leaves of the olive tree like a thick blanket — she was so bowed down with the weight that her branches bent and broke. But the snowflakes fell harmlessly through the bare branches of the fig, which survived for many more harvests.

People who boast about their wealth or their fortune can meet with unexpected disaster.

Mercury
and the
Woodman

Long, long ago in the early days of the world, the messenger god Mercury was walking through a forest when he heard someone groaning and moaning nearby. He hurried through the trees and found that the voice belonged to a woodman. The woodman had been felling a tree on the riverbank, when his axe had bounced off the trunk, flown out of his hands and fallen into the water. Now he stood by the water's edge lamenting his loss.

Mercury felt very sorry for the woodman. How

would he make a living without the tool of his trade? To the woodman's huge surprise, the god suddenly dived into the river. No sooner had Mercury plunged into the water than he reappeared – holding a golden axe.

"Is this what you lost?" he asked the woodman.

The woodman was of course tempted for a moment to reply that the amazing axe was his – but being an honest fellow he sighed, and did not.

Then Mercury dived a second time and brought up a silver axe, and asked if it was the woodman's.

"No, that is not mine either," said the woodman with another deep sigh.

Once more Mercury dived into the river, and this time he brought up the woodman's missing axe. The woodman was overjoyed at recovering his property, and thanked the god heartily. In turn, Mercury was so pleased with the woodman's honesty that he made him a present of the other two axes.

The woodman couldn't believe it. He hurried home and told the story to his friends – who were of course filled with envy. One of them was so jealous that he was determined to try his luck for himself.

The man went to the edge of the river and began to fell a tree, and presently let his axe drop into the water. Mercury appeared as

before, and on learning that the axe had fallen in, he dived and again brought up a golden axe.

Without waiting to be asked if it was his or not the man cried, "That's mine, that's mine!" and stretched out his hand eagerly for the prize. But Mercury was so disgusted at his dishonesty that he not only took away the golden axe, he also refused to recover the one that had fallen into the river.

Honesty is the best policy.

The Boy and the Nuts

There was once a little boy who noticed a jar of nuts on a shelf. They looked so tasty that he couldn't resist reaching up and lifting them down. He took off the lid, thrust his hand inside the jar, and greedily grasped as many as he could hold.

But when he tried to pull his hand out again, he found he couldn't, for the neck of the jar was too small to allow such a large handful to get through. The little boy didn't want to let go of all his tasty treats, but unless he did, he couldn't

get his hand out. The little boy burst into tears. Just then a neighbor was passing by the window and saw what the trouble was. "There, there," she said. "Come, my boy, don't be so greedy. If you let go of some of the nuts and be content with just half of what you have, you'll be able to get your hand out easily enough."

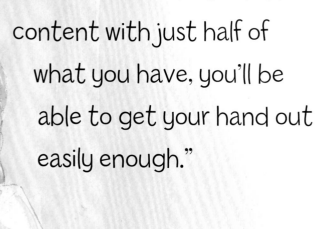

Do not attempt too much at once.

The Travelers and the Sycamore Tree

Two travelers were walking along a dusty road on a hot summer's day. They were relieved when they came across a broad sycamore tree, and turned off the road to shelter from the sun in the deep shade of its branches. They sank down and cooled off, and then got out some food to eat.

As the travelers rested, refreshed, they looked up into the tree. One of them remarked to his companion, "What a useless tree the sycamore is. It bears no fruit and is of no

service to
man at all."
Then the sycamore tree
interrupted him with great
indignation. "You ungrateful creature!" it
cried. "You come and take shelter beneath
me from the scorching sun, and then, in the
very act of enjoying the cool shade I
provide, you claim I am good for nothing!"

*Many a service is met
with ingratitude.*

The Sick Deer

A mighty deer was once the lord of the forest, held in awe and respected by all the other creatures that lived there.

However there came a time when the deer fell ill. He became so sick that he collapsed in a shady clearing, too weak to move from the spot. The birds flying overhead soon saw what had happened and talked about it in sadness. Soon other creatures heard too, and as the news of the deer's illness spread, many of the other forest beasts came to see how he was.

However as they came, they all nibbled a little of the grass that grew around the deer until there was not a blade within his reach.

After a few days the deer felt better, but by then he was too weak to go in search of food. And so it was that he died of hunger – due to the thoughtlessness of his friends.

Bad friends can do you more harm than good.

The Thief and the Innkeeper

O nce upon a time, a thief rented a room at an inn, and stayed there several days on the look-out for something to steal. However, no opportunity presented itself, until one day when the innkeeper appeared in a fine new coat.

The thief no sooner set eyes upon the coat than he longed to get his hands on it, so he took a seat in the garden by the innkeeper's side. They chatted amiably for some time, then the thief suddenly yawned and howled like a wolf.

The innkeeper was shocked and concerned,

and asked the thief what the matter was.

The thief replied, "I will tell you about myself, sir, but first I must beg you to take charge of my clothes for me, for I intend to leave them with you. Why I have these fits of yawning I cannot tell — maybe they are sent as a punishment for things I have done wrong. But the facts are that when I have yawned three times I become a raging wolf and fly at men's throats." As he finished speaking he yawned a second time and howled again as before.

The innkeeper, believing every word and terrified at the prospect of being confronted with a wolf, started to run indoors, but the thief caught him by the coat, crying, "Stay, sir, and take charge of my clothes, or I shall never see them again." As the thief spoke he opened his mouth and began to yawn for the third time.

The innkeeper, mad with fear, slipped out of his coat – which remained in the other's hands – and bolted inside. The thief then stole off with his spoil.

Don't always believe everything people say.

The Blackbird
and the
Hunter

A hungry blackbird once came across a myrtle bush covered in bright, juicy berries. She happily flew down and began to eat, hardly able to believe her luck. The little bird ate berry after berry until she was quite full. But she couldn't stop because the berries were so delicious!

The blackbird was so busy plucking off the berries that she didn't notice a bird-catcher, or fowler, approaching. He spotted the plump little bird at once and his eyes sparkled. Quickly and quietly, he took out some long reeds he had brought with him and spread them with sticky bird lime. Then, still unnoticed, he poked the reeds into the myrtle bush.

Of course, it was only a matter of time before the blackbird hopped onto one of the sticky reeds, and she was caught fast.

Immediately, the blackbird realized she was about to be killed.

"How foolish I am!" cried the blackbird pitifully, as the bird-catcher approached. "For the sake of a little pleasant food I have given up my life."

A moment's pleasure can bring a lifetime's misery.